The Adventures of Tootsie Turtle and Dobbie Doo

The Tattletale

Debbie Schrick

Illustrated by Doug and Suzi Bond

This is a work of fiction. All of the characters, names, incidents, organizations, and dialogue in this novel are either the products of the author's imagination or are used fictitiously.

WestBow Press books may be ordered through booksellers or by contacting:

WestBow Press
A Division of Thomas Nelson & Zondervan
1663 Liberty Drive
Bloomington, IN 47403
www.westbowpress.com
844-714-3454

Interior Image Credit: Doug and Suzi Bond

ISBN: 978-1-6642-5111-3 (SC)
ISBN: 978-1-6642-5112-0 (e)

Library of Congress Control Number: 2021924134

Print information available on the last page.

WestBow Press rev. date: 12/08/2021

WestBow
PRESS®
A DIVISION OF THOMAS NELSON
& ZONDERVAN

For my fun-loving and
encouraging Andrea.
You've always kept me laughing.
I love you Sweetie!

For our son, Jesse, with love.

Tootsie was a turtle,
A friend to everyone.
She got invited places,
'Cause she was so much fun.

Dobbie was a duckling,
Who waddled as she went.
She waddled close to Tootsie,
And with Toots, much time she spent-

One day Toots got a note
  From a friend so kind and true.
    It was from Ornery Orangutan,
    And she was turning two.

    "The note says it's her birthday,"
  Said Toots to Dobbie Doo.
  "She's going to have a party,
And you're invited too."

"Oh, a birthday party!
That sounds like lots of fun!
You told me about last year,
When she was turning one."

"Well, we better wrap a present,
Since Ornery's turning two.
Dob, don't give any hints…

...not even a single clue."

So, Toots and Dob went on their way,
To Ornery's house they went.
So many of their other friends,
Were also a card sent.

There was Bert Beaver,
Morty Mole, and Squeaky Squirrel too.

6

Jear Bear and Ollie Owl
In Ollie's rocket flew.

Everyone was having fun
'til Squeak's feelings were hurt.
And then she started tattling
On everyone—**even Bert!**

"Bert won't tie his shoe.
I don't like the look on Mort's face.
Ollie's going to trip me,
And Dobbie's out of place."

"I'm sure Jear Bear did something wrong,
And don't forget Ornery either!
You all make me so mad,
And I won't play with Toots neither."

Said Toots, "Squeaky, what's wrong?
You can tell me that.
Let's take it one problem at a time,
Sit here upon the mat."

So Squeaky continued tattling,
She told on everyone.
The party got really quiet,
And then wasn't any fun.

After listening, Toots told her,
"Think really keen.
Did anyone truly hurt you?
Or say anything that's mean?"

"Well," squeaked Squeaky
In her high-pitched sound,
"Ornery made a joke about tails,
And mine's the biggest around."

"I didn't mean to hurt you Squeak.
I just think tails are funny.
See, I don't have one,
And neither does my mummy."

Toots said, "We're all different.
That's why life's so great.
If everyone were the same,
A dull life that would make."

"So Ornery, you need to be careful,
That your words don't sting your friends.
Think before you speak.
Now with Squeaky make amends."

"I'm sorry Squeak, forgive me."
Said Ornery so sincere.

"I'll try to think before I speak,
But that's very hard I fear."

"And Squeaky there's something
You really need to know.
No one likes to play with others
Who tattle on them so."

Said Squeak, "They really bug me.
They hurt my feelings too.
When someone says something unkind,
Whatever shall I do?"

"I know that is a problem," said Toots.
"I'm sorry that you're hurt.
I'll tell you something that I learned,
From my very good friend Bert."

"When you're hurt, you can say,
'Maybe you didn't know
That when you say this or that
It hurts my feelings so'."

"What if they laugh at me,
And kick me in the shin?
Whatever shall I do?
What do I do then?"

"Then go and tell a grown-up.
No one should hurt you so,
Tell a trusted grown-up,
Someone that you know."

"But then aren't I tattling?
You said that isn't cool.
Sometimes my feelings get hurt
By bullies there at school."

"If you can talk to your friends
When something isn't right.
You'll find sometimes you've misunderstood,
And you can avoid a fight."

"If that doesn't work,
And they meant to hurt you so,
Go and tell a grown-up,
One you really know."

"I guess I didn't need to
Tell you about Bert's shoe.
And I can't really read Ollie's mind,
But that I guess you knew."

"I'm sorry Mort.
I know that's just your look.
You didn't mean anything by it.
It's my fault—the offense I took."

Then Squeaky asked,

"Can we play some more?
I love Ornery's jokes—it's true.
Especially the one about slippers,
And bananas that she threw."

Said Jear, "Oh that's a good one.
Though I really don't know why.
Maybe it's because the joker,
Is just a Sweetie Pie."

So, the friends all made up,
They said sorry for things they'd said.
They went home,
Said goodnight...

And
   Toots
      tucked
         Dob
           in bed.

Animal Fun Facts

Orangutans

- Size: Males are generally about 4 feet tall and females 3 feet tall.
- Weight: Males 130-200 pounds and females 90-110 pounds
- Mature at 8-10 years old
- Babies are born 260-270 days after the mother has mated. They live mostly alone with the exception of mothers and their young.
- They eat tropical fruits, leaves, bark, insects, and eggs.
- They live on the islands of Borneo and Sumatra in the tropical rainforest.
- They mostly live in the trees.
- They are active during the daytime.
- Females and the young orangutans sleep in nests in the trees at night.
- The adult males seem to prefer to sleep on the ground at night, because they are heavier.
- They live to about 35 years of age.
- They are an endangered animal.
- A female will usually only give birth every 3-6 years.
- Usually only one baby is born at a time. Very rarely twins are born.
- Babies weigh about 5 pounds when they are born.
- Babies are totally dependent on their mothers for the first 18 months.
- Babies travel by clinging on to their mother as she goes.
- Baby orangutans become more independent around 3 years of age, but they stay with their mother until she gives birth again.
- Communication: "They squeak and whine. Adult males make long, bubbling calls and they roar also."

(Information about orangutans was taken from the Wildlife Fact File.)
"Orangutans." Wildlife Fact File Card # 22 MCMXCI: International Masters Publishers